TOBY TUCKER

Mucking about with Monkeys

Also by Val Wilding

Toby Tucker: Keeping Sneaky Secrets

Toby Tucker: Dodging the Donkey Doo

Toby Tucker: Sludging through a Sewer

Toby Tucker: Picking People's Pockets

Toby Tucker: Hogging all the Pig Swill

TOBY TUCKER

Mucking about with Monkeys

VAL WILDING

Illustrated by Michael Broad

EGMONT

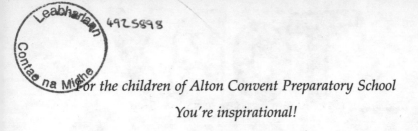

For the children of Alton Convent Preparatory School

You're inspirational!

EGMONT

We bring stories to life

Published in Great Britain 2007
by Egmont UK Limited
239 Kensington High Street, London W8 6SA

Text copyright © 2007 Val Wilding
Illustrations copyright © 2007 Michael Broad

The moral rights of the author and illustrator have been asserted

ISBN 978 1 4052 1839 9

1 3 5 7 9 10 8 6 4 2

A CIP catalogue record for this title is available
from the British Library

Printed and bound in Great Britain by the CPI Group

The Allen house, present day

Toby Tucker was so excited he could hardly eat. 'Did you say dog?' he asked. 'We're having a dog?'

'For a while,' said Evie, his foster mother. 'Only if Don agrees.'

'He will! He always agrees with you.'

That was almost true. Toby's foster father, Don, was one of the easiest people in the world to get along with, but when he felt strongly about something, he always spoke his mind.

'Anyway,' said Toby. 'It's your mum's dog, and she's going into hospital, so we have to have it. What's it like?'

It was only a couple of months since Toby had left the children's home to live with the Allens. He hadn't yet met the rest of the family. Don and Evie had moved into their house just before Toby arrived, and all their spare time was taken up with decorating and repairs.

Before Evie could reply, Don came in carrying a bag of nails.

'Hi both,' he said. 'Aren't you eating those sausages, Toby? Why not? Evie over-cooked them again? Can I borrow one to bang these nails in?' He took a sausage, bit into it and grinned at Evie. She stuck her tongue out.

Toby pinned his last sausage with a fork. Evie never overcooked anything!

'We're having a dog!' he said.

'We're not,' said Don. 'Flipping nuisances, they are. Always needing walks, shedding hairs everywhere, biting postmen, forever after food . . .'

'Apart from the postmen,' said Evie, 'that sounds just like you.' She put sausages, onions, green beans and mash in front of Don. 'Toby's right – we're having a dog, but not for long.'

'It's one of her mum's dogs,' Toby explained. 'What's it called, Evie?'

'Snowball.'

Toby thought Snowball was a fun name. 'While Evie's mum's having her hip done,' he continued, 'her neighbour's looking after one dog, and we're looking after Snowball.'

'Are we indeed?' said Don.

'If you agree,' Toby and Evie chorused.

Don frowned. 'I've never seen Snowball. It must be new. I suppose it won't be as much bother as the other one, that mad Barney.'

Toby jumped up. 'Hooray! We're getting a dog! Can I go and tell Jake and Amber?'

'Of course,' said Evie. 'Don't be late back.'

Toby didn't intend being late. He had something special to do.

Jake and Amber were thrilled about Snowball. 'It'll be nice for you,' said Jake. 'You

haven't got much of your own, so having a dog
will give you something to do.'

'Jake!' said Amber crossly.

'Ignore him,' said Toby. 'Jake, I keep telling
you, I've got loads of stuff.'

'But you only had clothes and a wooden chest
when you came to live with the Allens,' said Jake.
'You said the chest has nothing in it except –'

'For goodness' sake,' said Amber. 'The Allens
have bought Jake everything he needs.'

'Except a bike, and I'm saving up for that,' said

Toby. 'Anyway, I won't need a bike while Snowball's with us.' He grinned. 'I'll be walking my dog!'

'I'm back!' Toby yelled. 'Jake and Amber are coming round to see Snowball tomorrow.'

From the kitchen he heard Don's shocked, 'Tomorrow!' and Evie saying, 'Didn't I say? I'm fetching Snowball tomorrow. Coffee, dear?'

Toby giggled and went up to his room at the top of the house. He looked round. He certainly did have loads of stuff now – CD player, a TV that only played DVDs, because it didn't have a proper aerial, posters, clothes, great trainers, books, football fanzines – all sorts. Jake hadn't seen any of it for one good reason. The Allens were taking a long time getting round to decorating his room, and there was no way Toby was letting his mates see that he slept surrounded by pink fairy wallpaper.

The most important thing in the room stood beneath the window – his wooden chest. It held an incredible secret.

Toby opened it, felt beneath heaps of paper scraps and pulled out a framed photo. He believed it held a clue to the question that no one knew the answer to.

Who's Toby Tucker?

He got the same warm feeling he always did when he looked at the elderly man in the photo – that gentle face. 'Who are you?' Toby wondered. He read again the pencilled note on the back of the frame.

> The paper in the chest is your family tree. I wonder which little baby tore it up, eh, Toby Tucker? Piece it together and you'll find out who you are and when you come from.
>
> Gee.

Anyone reading that would think, as Toby once thought, that 'Gee', whoever he was, had made a mistake, writing 'when you come from' instead of 'where'. But now Toby knew differently.

He looked up at his pinboard on the wall. There were three names there already. With luck,

Toby would add a fourth tonight. All I need do to start the magic, he thought, is piece together a name from my family tree. He knew that was easier said than done. It was a fortnight since he'd last managed it. Tonight he felt lucky!

Suddenly, there was a yell.

'Tobeeee! Quick! Don's trying to paper the bedroom ceiling and all he's papered is himself!'

Toby sighed, put the photo back, and went downstairs to the Allens' bedroom. He couldn't help laughing. Don stood on a step ladder, with a sheet of wallpaper draped over his head. Paste dripped from it.

Evie handed Toby a broom. 'Once Don's stuck one end up, use that to hold it in place as he does the other end.' She turned to Don. 'If that doesn't work, I'm sticking it up with drawing pins!'

As Toby hoisted his broom, he thought of the wooden chest. Maybe tomorrow.

Toby raced home after school next day, dying to see Snowball! Jake and Amber were coming later, so they could all take the dog for a walk.

'Evie?' he called.

'In here!'

Toby threw his bag down and went to the kitchen. He stared.

'Hi,' said Evie. 'Meet Snowball.'

Toby couldn't believe his eyes. 'What's *that*?'

8

'Isn't she cute?' said Evie. 'Wait till Don sees her!'

Yeah, Toby thought grimly. Just wait.

Snowball was small, white and unbelievably fluffy. Thoughts of going for walks and playing in the park vanished from Toby's mind. He wasn't being seen out with *that*.

The front door slammed, and Don shouted, 'Well, where is it?'

'Here,' said Toby, in a dull voice.

Don came in. 'You don't sound very thrilled –' He stopped. 'That's a dog? That's not a dog. It's a – a – hot water bottle cover.' He looked at Evie hopefully. 'Isn't it?'

Evie scooped Snowball into her arms. 'She is a dog, and she's lovely,' she said, crossly. 'Aren't you, little doggy foo foo?'

Don turned away in disgust. 'Little doggy foo foo, my foot,' he said. 'Well, Toby, you wanted a dog. You going to take it for a walk?'

'Her,' Evie muttered.

9

'No way,' said Toby. 'I've got homework.'

'On a Friday night?' said Evie. 'You never do homework on a Friday night. Take Snowball for a walk. Both of you!'

She thrust a lead into Don's hands. He thrust it into Toby's. 'You wanted a dog,' he said, opening the front door. 'You hold it.'

'Not a chance,' said Toby. 'Imagine if my mates saw me with this ball of fluff!'

Don laughed. 'Too late, lad.'

Jake and Amber were coming up the path.

'They can go with you,' said Don with a pleased grin. He went in, shutting the door firmly behind him.

Jake flatly refused to be seen with 'that cotton-wool ball on legs', but Amber thought Snowball was sweet, and took her for a walk while the boys sat on a wall and grumbled.

Don and Evie went to the DIY store on Saturday morning, and then to the hospital to see Evie's mum. They left Toby in charge of Snowball.

Toby decided to spend the morning trying to piece together a new name from his family tree. He went to his room, opened the chest and took out an armful of paper scraps, which he dumped on the deep red carpet.

'I must be able to get a name out of this lot,' he said, settling with his back against the bed.

The first pieces he tried were useless. 'Reg . . . ola . . . Sch . . .' He picked out another. 'John . . .'

'John? John!' It was the first time he'd ever pulled out a complete name. Toby laid it on the carpet and waited.

Nothing.

Had the magic gone?

Skkr skkr skkr. What was that? Toby ignored the sound, and smoothed the paper out. Nothing.

Skkr skkr skkr.

'That flipping dog!' Toby opened the door, and there was Snowball, gazing up at him.

'Go downstairs,' Toby said angrily. The dog didn't move. 'All right,' he said, 'if you want to stay there, stay. Stay!'

Obediently, Snowball lay down.

Toby went back to the pile of paper pieces and 'John'.

He looked up at his pinboard. The first three people didn't have surnames. Maybe this one did.

Toby searched frantically through the scraps. 'It must have a capital. Rol . . . Bunn . . .'

Bunn?

Holding his breath, because he knew exactly what might happen, Toby put the two pieces together.

John Bunn.

The magic began. A drawing of a boy in a dirty shirt and short baggy trousers, a bit like knickers, appeared on the paper. Just as before, it morphed into a picture of Toby himself. His tummy always did roly-polys when that happened. The picture changed back into the boy and a strange silvery light shimmered over it.

Toby stood up. The shimmering light grew, higher than his head, then moved towards and over him. The familiar feeling of cold jelly slipping through his body came and went, and Toby knew that when he turned round, he would see –

The boy in the short baggy trousers!

Toby waited, knowing he was about to be drawn by a great power, like a strong magnet, towards the boy.

He felt the powerful tug, and struggled to stay on his feet. 'Look out! I'm coming!' he cried, but he couldn't keep upright!

Toby tumbled forward – crash! - into the boy, and on to something soft, and very, very smelly.

'Whoo!' he said, sitting up. 'What was that noise? Sounded like someone crashing through something.'

He blinked. 'I can't remember who I am.' He rubbed his eyes. 'No, I know who I am all right. I'm

John – John Bunn. But where am I?' His eyes slowly focussed.

He was in bed. And in there with him were lots of tiny, hopping fleas.

1542, London

Good old Mother Moody! There is to be an execution today. I have not seen one for months, and if Mother Moody had not fallen through the stairs, I might never have woken in time!

I had slept heavily, and my sleep was filled with strange dreams. I cannot remember them clearly, but I do know that when I did wake, the words, 'look out! I'm coming!' were ringing in my ears, and I felt most odd.

But then I remembered that all I have to do this morning is go to the Tower of London, make sure the animals have water, then find a quiet corner to watch the execution. Huzzah! Five hours with no lion dung!

But Mother Moody was in trouble, so first I had to get up and help her! She lives in the attic room opposite ours. She is not my mother (who is dead), but that is what everyone calls her. She is kind, but forgetful. Today she forgot to count the stairs. We have to do that because they are mostly rotten, and it is important to know which ones to jump. Mother Moody cannot jump. Her legs are too short. Instead, she seems to roll over the broken ones – today she made a mistake.

After I had pulled Mother Moody free and helped her downstairs, she said, 'John Bunn, I shall bring you home a piece of gingerbread. You are a good lad, though you stink.'

I laughed. 'I cannot help that,' I replied. 'It's

my work.'

She snorted. 'You should not be shovelling animal muck and spreading it on rich people's gardens, even if it is from the king's own beasts. You should be in charge of the animals. You have a gift, John Bunn. Animals trust you.'

So they do. But muck shovelling and spreading is my job. King Henry is sometimes given wild animals by foreign kings. They are kept in the Royal Menagerie in the Lion Tower at the Tower of London. That is where I work, with Master Scrope.

Scrope is quick with his tongue and his stick. Sometimes he taunts the lions, for fun. I should like to let loose Henry, our fiercest lion, and see who has fun then!

Not even Scrope can spoil today. Everyone

wonders what will happen. The last person exe-cuted in the Tower was the Countess of Salisbury. She refused to lay her head on the block! The exe-cutioner had to chase her around the scaffold, hacking at her, while she screamed that she was innocent. Today will be different. The person being beheaded is the queen!

I have never seen Queen Catherine, but she is young and beautiful, they say. She has been mar-ried to King Henry for less than two years. Her crime was to have gentleman friends when she should have been faithful to the king. That is trea-son, and her punishment is death.

Next day

We had two executions yesterday, not one! The queen's lady-in-waiting, Jane Rochford, was accused of helping her meet men friends, so she got the chop, too.

I found a place beside the Tower blacksmith,

but he pushed me away, saying I stink of dung, so I moved out of sniffing distance.

Black cloth hung round the scaffold, and it was strewn with clean straw, to mop up the blood. The executioner was waiting to kneel and ask the queen's forgiveness. It's best to forgive him, so he tries to chop your head off with one blow. The quicker the better.

The queen could hardly walk. If it were me about to die, I think I would faint. But she was brave at the end and made a speech saying she had done wrong. That made tears come to my eyes and I had to wipe my nose on my sleeve. She looked so small.

As the queen put her head on the block, her ladies howled their eyes out. Then – chop – it was done. Lady Rochford was next. They say she went mad in the last weeks, but she looked normal enough to me as she put her head down. The last thing she ever saw was a pool of her mistress's blood.

The queen's body was taken to St Peter's, the Tower church, to be buried next to another beheaded queen, Anne Boleyn. King Henry does not keep his wives well, I think. I dare not say so aloud, in case I end up a prisoner myself.

I hurried back to work. Although the Lion Tower is part of the Tower of London, it is actually outside the Tower walls.

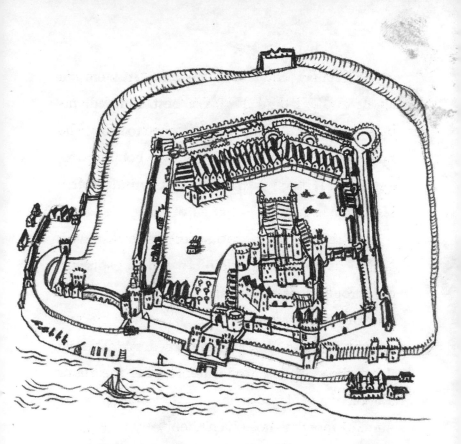

So I work on the west side of the Tower, and I live at St Katherine's on the east. I am usually late.

The first thing that greeted me was angry squawking. It was Pooper the parrot. Only the king's beasts should be in the menagerie, but Scrope won Pooper in a dice game with a blind sailor. (He couldn't lose!) He hates the parrot now,

21

because it likes me best and will not go to him.

Pooper does not mind that I smell of dung. He knows lots of sailors' swear words, and is often rude – especially to Scrope. That makes me laugh, but it makes Scrope box my ears.

Scrope also won two monkeys, which I love. I call them Tittle and Tattle, because the sound they make is like tittle-tattle – they chatter all the time. Scrope has not given them names. To him they are only a way of earning extra money.

He slides up to visitors and offers to show them something special for an extra penny.

Then he takes them into the monkey room to see the monkeys at play. The ladies especially like that.

I fed Pooper chunks of apple. Scrope came in and caught me, but the first I knew of it was a whack across my leg with his stick. It has a sharp nail driven into one end, and he uses it to poke the animals. He calls it his prodder and says it makes them fear him. That is probably a good thing with the lions, but he has made Pooper, Tittle and Tattle fear him, too. I would hate them to fear me. They're fun. And they like me, which no one else does, because of my stink.

Only my father does not mind the stink because, since he was wounded, he cannot smell anything.

Father was once a handsome, brave soldier, but he was badly injured in a fight with some drunken men. Now he cannot get work, because

23

people do not like to look at him. He is always sad. Sometimes he stays in bed all day. Sometimes he begs in the street, then spends the money in a tavern. My sister Bessie says if he tidied his hair and beard, and did not sleep in his jerkin, he would not look so bad and might get work.

Scrope made me spend the whole afternoon scrubbing the yard in the middle of the Lion Tower. That means someone important is coming.

At dusk I made my way home. As I passed through the Postern Gate, I nearly collapsed with fright when a small shape hurtled at me out of the darkness.

It was Nellie!

'John Bunn, when can I see the lions?' she cried. 'I hear them roar, but what do they look like?'

Nellie is a pest. She lives next door to me, and I have known her since she was small. She is like a naughty puppy, always chasing after me.

'I cannot let you in when Master Scrope is there,' I told her. 'One day, Nellie, one day.' I took her home. Her family is large, and her mother had not noticed Nellie was missing. She never does.

I am tired tonight and was glad to find that Bessie had been with a plate of leftover venison pasty for Father and me. A treat!

Today I cleaned out the animal cages all morning.

We use a pulley to raise the cage bars. Scrope pokes the animals so they go on to their upper levels, while I scrape out their droppings, which

are large and plentiful. I shovel it all on my barrow, and wheel it to our steaming manure heap. From there, I take it to people's gardens. I collect money for the dung and give it to Scrope.

Scrope calls himself the animal keeper, which indeed he is. But Master Ralph Worsley has the title Keeper of the King's Menagerie, though he does no work at all. King Henry gave him the title, and a lovely house in the corner of the Lion Tower. Master Worsley will have the title until he dies – as long as he doesn't upset the king! That goes for many of the king's courtiers. The king is bad-tempered, they say, because his leg hurts him. It's diseased. He used to be called Bluff King Hal because he was a hearty man. I think he should be called Grumpy King Hal.

It was Master Worsley who came today. He was wearing silk hose, not ordinary wool, and he had a travelling cloak on that was lined with fur – more fur than a lion has on its whole body! And he had an ostrich feather in his cap. The ostrich must be a beautiful, graceful bird to have such lovely plumage.

Master Worsley did not even glance at the animals, but passed by with a cloth pressed to his nose. I would love fine clothes. I would like it if people walked past me and did not say, 'Pyaugh!'

'All that scrubbing, and he hardly noticed,' I grumbled to Scrope.

'He would have noticed if he'd had to wade through the piles of dung you drop from your barrow,' Scrope snapped. 'Dolt!'

As usual, 'Dolt!' was accompanied by a whack on the ear, and an echoing 'Dolt!' from Pooper.

It has taken all week to catch up on my work. Everything was behind because of the executions and Master Worsley's visit. On Friday he brought a group of rich friends round to gape at the animals.

Scrope was most anxious not to let Master Worsley see the monkeys, so he shut me up with them and told me to keep them quiet. That was like trying to catch a grasshopper in the wind – hardly possible. But I did my best and was glad, when I was let out, to see that Master Worsley had gone.

'He did not hear the monkeys, then?' I asked.

'No, but he heard the parrot,' Scrope barked. 'It called him "dolt!" What have you been teaching it, you dizzard?'

Another clout on my head. I nearly fell over.

I hate this place. I like the animals – even the fierce ones – but I can't stand Scrope, and he does not like me. I don't want to work here any more.

Today Africa, the she-lion, ripped Master Scrope's arm with her claw. It was his fault. She was perfectly quiet until he jabbed her in the belly with his prodder. I ran – not too fast – for the Tower physician, but he was busy attending to a prisoner who had tried to kill himself. I have seen some of the places prisoners are kept, and I too would wish to die if I were there.

Scrope sent me to the apothecary for a salve for his arm. As I left the Tower, little Nellie attached herself to me, and would not go away.

I waited outside the shop until other customers had gone. I knew that if I went in, there would be great sniffs and grumbles before I was kicked out.

When everyone had left, I sat Nellie on the ground outside and went in.

'Ah, 'tis you, John Bunn!' said the apothecary, a nice old gentleman. 'No, no! Stand at the door, please. What is it?'

'A salve for a lion scratch, please,' I said. 'For Master Scrope.'

Nellie's voice chirped, 'Horrible gong-head!'

I would like to be an apothecary and make

people well. Then I would not be called 'dolt' or 'dizzard'. I would be known as Master Bunn.

The apothecary made a mixture in his pestle and mortar, muttering, "Twill sting a good deal, but the cut, if not too deep, will mend. If it does not, Master Scrope must visit the barber.'

I took the salve and we hurried back to the Tower. As I left Nellie at the gate, she shouted, 'I hope it hurts!' I hoped so, too. It cheered me to know that it would sting. But if Scrope does have to visit the barber-surgeon, I do not envy him.

I hope I never have to visit a barber-surgeon. They are always pulling out teeth or cutting people up.

Scrope went home early, so I looked down by
the river for Nellie's cousin, Dan. When he saw
me, he rowed to shore and picked me up. We
went to the middle of the river, pulled the oars in,
and bobbed on the water, chatting. I told Dan how
much I hate Scrope. He said Scrope is a vicious
snake who should be roasted and fed to the lions.

Then Dan said, 'Why not leave the Tower and
be a waterman like me?'

'Because,' I said, 'you inherited your father's

boat. My father only has a bed, and I wouldn't get far on that!'

But, I thought later, I could try and find another job. One that would not make me smell.

Scrope's arm still hurts a week later. I suggested he should stay in his bed for a day or two. 'Fool!' he said. 'Suppose King Henry decided to visit his beasts and found them in the care of a stupid boy – a boy so loose in the head that he is only fit to shovel dung!'

King Henry hardly ever visits. And I am not fit only to shovel dung. I will prove it one day. All I need is a chance.

My sister Bessie visited us after church yesterday. She had the whole afternoon off.

She works in the house of the Lord Lieutenant of the Tower. It is only two years old, and very grand inside, Bessie says. She will show me it one day. Sometimes Bessie helps the cook, sometimes she does laundry, and sometimes she cleans the house.

Father was miserable and, as usual, Bessie made it worse by nagging him to make himself look nice and go out looking for work. 'You must try to smile more, too,' she said.

I thought Father was going to knock her through the wall. I'm sure he only stopped himself because he needs the food and money she brings.

'Smile?' he roared. 'Smile? Look at me, girl!'

Then he did smile. He is not handsome now, and it is worse when he smiles because only one side of his face moves.

Bessie cried then, so I tried to cheer her up. 'I'm going to the Lord Lieutenant's house on Tuesday to spread muck on his garden,' I said. 'Shall I take Pooper, to make the cook laugh? Perhaps he will swear at the steward!'

Bessie laughed at the thought of Pooper, and Father smiled his crooked smile, and we all guzzled the ham and bread that Bessie had brought.

34

She and the other servants eat lovely food. Sometimes the cook gives Bessie extra for her family – us! I once told Bessie to tell the cook her father has a pig at home, then maybe she would

send more food. Bessie said, 'I cannot lie – Father has no pig.' 'He has,' I replied. 'Me!'

When I went to the Lord Lieutenant's house today, I took such a huge load of muck it fairly dripped off my barrow. It took hours to spread, and I knew I would be in trouble with Scrope for taking too long. Pooper kept his beak shut, so I had no little treat from the cook. A waste of time and good muck.

'I'll bring food tomorrow,' said Bessie. 'Here.' She gave me money to buy a meat pie for supper.

I worked hard all afternoon. On top of my own jobs, I had to run errands for Scrope, because his arm is flaming red and sore. Ha! Every time I went near him, I made sure I knocked into it. Then I said, 'Sorry!' and scurried away before he had time to grab his prodder.

Scrope is well now, and as bad-tempered as ever, which meant trouble for me today. He went to the meat market in Eastcheap first thing. His friend in a slaughterhouse there sells him meat at a good

price. Once Scrope's deal is done, the meat is delivered weekly, but the delivery man dumps it at the gate. The guards rage at Scrope, which I

like. His fault for paying low prices and keeping the rest of the money himself.

But it is poor John Bunn who must heave the stinking, slimy meat on to a barrow and wheel it in. By this time the beasts are going wild. They smell blood.

This morning, while Scrope was gone, I took Tittle and Tattle to the river for some fresh air. And who was waiting around outside? Nellie. She adores watching the monkeys, though she will not touch them.

Nellie sniffed. 'I can smell the sea, John Bunn.'

'How do you know?' I said. 'You have never seen the sea, so how do you know what it smells like?'

'I can smell it in my head,' she said.

Pooper rode on my shoulder, nibbling my hair and shouting, 'Scurvy villain!' into my ear.

Nellie asked, 'Why do the poor monkeys wear little collars? Why do you keep them on leads?'

'Because Scrope would skin me alive if I lost them.'

It's not that Scrope cares about the monkeys, but he does care about the money they earn him. I felt sure they would not run far from me, and would always return, but have always been afraid they might jump on a boat and be carried away.

But today the tide was low, and I could see that the monkeys were longing to get down to the water. I did not wish to trudge across the muddy shore, so I took a chance and let Tattle loose.

'The River Thames is the greatest river in the world, Nellie,' I said. 'I would like to be a sailor and travel the seven seas.'

'Seven!' she snorted in disbelief.

'Or perhaps I might be a spice merchant,' I went on. 'Then, when people sniffed me they'd love my smell, and I'd always have company. The only company I ever have is you, Bessie, and Father, who can smell nothing.'

'And the monkeys,' said Nellie. 'John Bunn . . . Look!'

One moment Tattle was picking at pebbles. The next – he was gone. Like lightning, he leapt and scrambled over mud, steps, boats, ropes.

Nellie called and I whistled, but he wouldn't come. Pooper screeched words that made even sailors look up in surprise.

My stomach turned like a butter churn. I told Nellie to hold Tittle, but she was afraid to.

'I'll take her back to the guards,' I told Nellie. 'If one of them will hold her lead, I'll be free to chase Tattle.' I ran along the wharf and turned up towards the Lion Gate. Tittle chattered madly.

Suddenly Pooper, behind me, screeched:

'Come 'ere, fool!', sounding just like Scrope! For a moment I thought I'd been caught out but, as I slid to a stop and turned, I saw Tattle running along behind us, chattering angrily. He ran up my leg and clung on to Tittle for dear life.

Thank goodness the monkeys are so used to being together. Tattle was afraid to be left alone.

I whistled for Pooper. But he'd flown ahead and was diving at someone by the gate, screeching: 'Slit yer throat, dolt!'

Scrope! His face flamed when he saw the monkeys were out, and he chased me all the way into the Lion Tower. I locked myself in with Tittle and Tattle until he'd calmed down, but he still took his stick to me when I came out – again and again he hit me.

I stopped on the way home and sat against a wall. My bruises ached. I was annoyed to see Nellie pop up from behind a tree stump, but she knew I'd be upset and simply curled up and snuggled against me. After a bit, I said, 'I hate

Scrope, Nellie. I like working with the beasts, but I do not want to work for that man any more. I must, though, until I find another job. Father and I cannot live on Bessie's leftovers. But who would give a job to a dung boy?'

'I would,' said Nellie. 'You smells lovely to me, John Bunn.' She threw her arms round me and squeezed. It hurt a lot, but I didn't say so.

I delivered two barrow-loads of lion dung to a school today. It is a fine place. The teachers' maids were doing the laundry, and one was making soap. Pooh! And they say I stink!

The midday meal was cold, as it was washing day, so I did not get my usual roast meat. Instead I had bread – not too fresh – some hard cheese and an orange, which I have never had before. I bit into it, and quickly spat. It was bitter. The scullery boy laughed and told me to pull off the skin. That was a messy task, but the inside was sweet, though stringy, and full of annoying pale seeds.

I took the cheese and bread and sat against the school wall, which was warm from the sun. I watched the maids screw up the sheets to squeeze the water out, then spread them over the ground and bushes to dry. It looked hard work.

My washing day's much quicker than theirs! Maybe I could ask the maid for a bit of soap, so I can make myself smell nice.

Through the window above me, a boy spoke in a foreign language. I knelt up and peeped in. It was a big schoolroom. I went to dame school when I was five – the dame was an old woman who gave lessons in her front room, which was tiny. She taught me to read and write. Then Father was injured and could not earn money, so I left. It did not matter. I learned quickly, and I know lots. But I do not know the things these boys know, like Latin and French. What will those boys do with all that learning? Maybe if I learned what they do, I could be something better than a muck-spreader. I am sure I could. A schoolmaster, perhaps!

I asked the maid for some soap. She screeched with laughter and said it would take more than that to make me sweet.

When I got back, I asked Scrope what school he went to.

'School of life, boy,' he said, and told me to get back to work.

I was in the city today, so I took my chance and looked for work.

I asked the turnkey at Newgate if he needed a boy to run errands. They sell food and candles to prisoners who have money. I thought I might fetch them. He laughed and said people brought food and candles to him to sell to prisoners. I tried the prison above Ludgate next. They told me to go and stink out someone else's place.

I told an onion seller that if two of us worked

we would sell twice as many. She said, 'If I give you a string of onions to sell, I'll never see you again. Do you think I am simple?'

The sweep said I wasn't fit to go into people's houses. 'You reek like a jakes in August!' he said.

Mention of the jakes reminded me I needed to pee so I headed for the Queenhithe privy.

Then I gave up job-hunting and went back to the Lion Tower. Scrope boxed my ears for being gone so long, and Pooper called me a drunken

poltroon, which is probably sailor-talk for someone not very nice.

Today I took dung to one of my favourite places –
a large house, owned by a rich merchant. Though
they have so much money, the merchant's family
are kind to people like me. The lady herself came
to give me Scrope's money. Not in my hand, of
course. No fine person comes near me. But she
stood at the kitchen door, put the coins in her gardener's hands, and nodded towards me.

I had to leave a little extra pile of dung by the
herb garden. The lady's mad about herbs, and

wants the gardener to manure the soil there himself, without getting dung on the plants.

I think I could be a gardener. I asked the lady, very respectfully, 'Madam, do you need a boy to help in your garden?'

She smiled and said that when she does want someone, she will think of me. I said, 'I can be found at the Tower, my lady, in the king's menagerie.'

'Indeed!' she said. Everyone laughed. They all know where I come from because I smell of lion and dung. I did not laugh.

Then the lady sent food and drink out to the gardener, and I was sent the same. It must be wonderful to work for someone who is nice to you. Scrope thinks of me as little more than one of the beasts.

London has been so hot lately that Scrope has decided the king is unlikely to visit for a while. Henry moves around his different palaces, and often stays with his noble friends. They say the king has to keep moving to give his servants a chance to clean up every now and then.

It's a blessing for me if the king is away, because it means Scrope stops twitching nervously every time he hears a band of horsemen approach, or a flurry of trumpets.

So today Scrope is visiting his mother. That is strange to me – I find it hard to believe that he was ever a small boy! He must have been glad when he was old enough to give up wearing dresses and start wearing breeches. Much easier to kick harmless creatures.

I made the most of the day. First, I looked for Nellie, to show her the lions, but she was nowhere to be seen. Dan's wherry was unmoving, way out in the middle of the river. I could see his hat, which meant he was asleep underneath it. I yelled to see if he knew where Nellie was, but he didn't stir. Then, as I made my way back up the hill to the gate, I was grabbed from behind! Nellie!

'I have been looking for you,' I said, laughing. 'Come and see the beasts!'

Nellie could not speak for excitement. When she saw the first she-lion, Africa, her little mouth hung open and her breath came fast. 'Will it bite me?' she whispered.

'She would gobble you up in one go,' I said. 'Watch.' I had extra food for the animals today, so I pushed chunks of meat between the cage bars. Nellie scuttled backwards as she saw how Africa tore at it.

I showed her our new wolf. He prowls about his small cage on long, thin legs.

'He looks as if he would like to run and run,'

said Nellie.

'The lions look lazy,' I said, 'but I think they would like to run, too. There must be lots of space where they come from, and tall trees, and maybe a river where they can drink – perhaps smaller than the Thames.'

Nellie glanced around and made a face. 'They cannot run here.'

'No,' I said, 'but if I was in charge, I would fill in the part of the moat that curves around the Lion Tower, and plant grass, and let all the animals run there in the sunshine. I would dig a pool for them to drink from, and swim in. Their fur would look good if it was clean.'

'You are kind, John Bunn,' said Nellie. 'You stink, but you're kind.'

Tomorrow Scrope will return, and the menagerie will be back to normal.

It's so hot. Even at nine in the evening, the air is stifling in our room. Father moans and tosses on his bed, complaining that he cannot sleep. I should think not. He hasn't moved from there all day, except to drink the ale I brought him at noon.

Scrope sent me into the city this morning to fetch some boots that were being repaired. Of course, Nellie followed me. Scrope had given me directions, but they were wrong, I am sure. We ended up in a maze of narrow lanes and alleys, where the houses almost shut out the light.

The whole area was poor – worse than St Katherine's, where Nellie and I live. It was noisy with talk and shouts, bursts of laughter, swearing and children crying. I had just decided to ask a 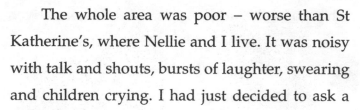 passing water carrier for directions, when there was a shout from above, and Nellie yelled, 'Watch out!'

I was too slow to look up. When I did, I saw the contents of a slop bucket falling towards me.

I dodged, but too late. The water carrier laughed and offered me a splash of water to clean my face.

'Though by the smell of you, it would take a river to wash you properly,' he said cheerfully.

I asked him if he knew where the shoemaker's workshop was.

He laughed at me! 'No shoemakers here, lad!' he said. 'Look around. There are hardly any shoes.'

It was true. Most people were barefoot.

'Best to move on,' he said. 'I'm only passing through. I wouldn't stop here.'

We took the water carrier's advice and moved on. In the end, I gave up looking for the shoemaker. I told Scrope the boots were not ready, and promised to fetch them tomorrow.

Next day

Scrope fetched the boots himself! I trembled all the time he was gone, for I knew he would discover I hadn't been to the shoemaker's. When he returned, he set about me with his stick.

I am so miserable. I would like to run away and be a water carrier, but I don't have money to buy a barrel. And what would Father do without me?

And now the lion called Henry (the king's lion, because he is named the same) is sick. We don't know what is wrong with him, but Scrope is very worried. Henry eats little, and his eyes are dull. Scrope eats little, too, and his eyes are scowling.

A week later

Henry is not eating. He lies so still. Scrope made me go into the cage to tip some water into the beast's mouth. I have never been so afraid in my life, but Scrope stood behind me with his stick and a menacing look on his face. I went in, clutching a cup of water, and knelt down. By St George! They think I smell bad! They should put their noses near a lion's jaws. My hand shook so badly that the water spilled over Henry's mouth. He did not move, but his tongue lapped gently when the cold water touched it.

The death of our Henry would be a bad sign. In the past, every lion named after a king has lived until the time of the king's death, and then it, too, has died. The king of beasts and the King of England are linked in some mysterious way.

Scrope fears either that the king is dying, or that he will go wild with fury (and fear) if he hears that his namesake has died.

Next evening, I was alone in the menagerie, apart from the beasts. Scrope ordered me to watch poor Henry, who we feared would not last the night. I could do nothing except dribble a little water into his mouth every now and then.

I went into the cage on my own. I was no longer afraid of Henry. I wished I could cure him, but I do not know how. The other beasts were silent. Did they know Henry was going to die? Do they have feelings, like us?

When I wasn't with Henry, I kept my eyes closed, in case I saw a ghost. Scrope says he has heard the ghostly screams of Countess Salisbury as the executioner chases her with his axe. I sang,

to keep bad noises out, and I took the monkeys some plums, so I had company for a while.

To pass the time, I taught Pooper to screech, 'Scrope's a doddypoll!' Well, he is – a complete blockhead.

Once the sky began to lighten, I looked forward to the sun rising to take the chill out of my cold bones. To warm myself, I went up on to the high walkway that overlooks the yard. From there I could see right across London.

At first I thought the sun was early, but then I realised that the glow I could see was a fire from someone's house! It's been so dry lately that it takes just one stray spark to set light

to thatch. I hoped the house dwellers kept a ladder and stack grab handy, so they could pull the burning thatch down. Otherwise, they might lose all.

A bellow from down below told me Scrope had arrived.

Henry the lion has died. He was so thin that it wasn't worth feeding his body to the other beasts. Anyway, Scrope wanted him out of sight as soon as possible, so we buried him. We had to drag his body on to a board, and pull him along like a convict going to Tyburn. The only trouble was, we didn't have horses to do the pulling, nor bystanders to urge us along.

So Henry was buried. But – abracadabra! We have a new Henry! Scrope says no one who matters ever gets near enough to the beasts to tell the difference. All we must do is make sure we can produce a lion named Henry.

We chose Samson, the lion that looked most

like the dead one, and Scrope said we must move him to Henry's cage. Even with Scrope's evil prodder poking the beast and hitting me, I knew that was dangerous.

'Samson might escape!' I warned.

'We must move him,' snarled Scrope. 'See, fool?' He pointed to the wooden name board nailed above Henry's cage. 'If he is to be "Henry", he must be in Henry's cage. Are you brainless?'

And he calls *me* 'fool'! I marched across and wrenched the wooden board off the wall. I strode back to Scrope and, with an artificial smile on my face, said, 'Master Scrope? Could we not move Henry's name board to Samson's cage?'

If it hadn't been such a good idea, he'd have knocked me from here to Whitehall for being so cheeky. But we moved the board, and I am ordered to tell everyone that Samson has died.

The curious thing is that I wonder now how true it is that kings and the lions named after them, die at the same time.

No matter. Scrope will have to be nice to me now, because I know the truth about Henry and Samson.

I was wrong! Scrope does not have to be nice to me. He proved that next day by grabbing my throat and saying, 'Breathe a word about Henry dying, boy, and you will be hanged for treason.'

Treason! The very word makes my guts twist as if I have swallowed a snake. I was glad when Scrope ordered me to take a message to the bear garden on the other side of the river. It meant I could escape from him for a while. I made my way along Thames Street and down New Fish Street to London Bridge.

I thought of what Scrope said this morning, and can imagine my own

head on a spike, like all the traitors'
heads high above the bridge.
Anyone who crosses into London
sees the heads, which are a warning to
all: do not be a traitor to the king, or your
head will be hacked off, boiled for a
while in the gatehouse,
then covered in tar to stop
it rotting away to bones!

Once I'd crossed the river to Southwark, I turned right, ran to the stinky stream in Dead Man's Place and cleared it in one jump. Before me was the bear baiting ring. I could tell by the shouts and cheers that there was a fight in progress. The bear garden man gave me a penny ha'penny for my trouble. On the way back, I passed a cottage where a woman sold food from her window. I bought a hot mutton pie, rich with gravy and, further along, a mug of ale. It was a good dinner!

Today we had our first important visitors since Henry died. Ordinary people have been, of course, but it does not matter what they think, because they have never seen the real Henry. They have probably never seen the real King Henry, come to that, which I have – from a distance. He was on a horse, amidst a cheering crowd, all shouting, 'Hurrah for good King Hal!' Poor horse – I'm surprised it didn't collapse!

Scrope greeted the visitors, bowing so low his nose nearly touched the ground. He took their money. 'Thank you, great lords,' he said in a whiny voice. 'This way, my lords and ladies.'

I waited near the door to the monkey room, as usual, while he showed them the wolf and the lions. As they examined the new Henry, Scrope clenched his fists. He does that when he is nervous. (And just before he thumps me.)

'Handsome indeed,' said one of the ladies, 'but it makes no sound.'

'And it does not move,' said another. 'What use is a beast that does not growl or prowl? You, there,' she said to Scrope, 'don't stand about like a simpering servant. Make it do something.'

Stupid woman. Of course it does not move. What is there to move for?

Scrope immediately slid his prodder between the bars and dug the lion in its side with the sharp nail. It snarled, and slashed at the stick with its great paw, but Scrope was too quick. I saw blood on the lion's fur.

He did not need to cut the lion to make it roar. If I take food to Samson – I mean Henry – he snarls instantly.

The party grew bored and made their way across the yard, looking for fresh creatures to amuse them. They found me.

'May I show you something special, my good lords and ladies?' Scrope bowed low and rubbed his dirty hands together.

I opened the door.

'Our amazing monkey room!' Scrope announced.

Tittle and Tattle get excited when the door opens, because they think it means food. Everyone loved watching them jump and swing.

One gentleman said, 'I am sure these creatures are favourites of the king!'

Scrope went red. 'Of course, my lord,' he said, bowing so low his hat fell off. 'Great favourites, they are.' He held out his hand. 'That will be another penny each, thank you, for seeing the monkeys play.'

As the gentleman paid, he murmured, 'I shall

mention to the king that we, too, have enjoyed his monkeys.'

Scrope went as white as a ship's sail. I felt happy.

Scrope has skulked about for a fortnight now, being extra nice to everybody (except me). He expects, any day, to hear that the king is demanding to know where the monkeys came from. I don't think the king will spare them a thought. Monkeys are not as important as running the country. Or choosing a new wife!

For that's what people think 'good King Hal' will do soon. Perhaps the king wants another boy, just in case Edward, his sickly son, dies. He has always been desperate to have sons.

We had four lots of visitors today. Scrope is

still scared to let anyone see the monkeys, so he's furious at missing out on four lots of extra money. And who suffers when he is angry? John Bunn.

Most visitors brought a dead animal, like a cat or a large rat, so they could visit the menagerie free. One brought a mouse! Does he think we can feed lions on mice? Scrope swung the mouse round by the tail and flung it over the wall. "Twould be more use to the apothecary than to a lion,' he grumbled.

It is cold tonight. Father dreads winter. The wind blows hard along the river, and we have no shutters at our window. Bessie will find some rags to stuff in the gap. I hate it when Father is miserable.

I've been thinking of what Scrope said about the mouse. It's given me an idea. I cannot wait to get to work to try it out!

I have earned four shillings! It's so easy. I set traps for mice, then I carry them to the apothecary, and

he pays me! I do not kill the mice. I'm not like
Scrope. I could not harm living creatures for no
reason. (Except wasps. I hate wasps.) But I know
the apothecary will use the mice to cure people.

Mouse innards can make a wart on the nose dis-
appear, and cure earache, and the apothecary said
mice can even be used to make your breath smell
nice! He bakes mouse heads in the oven till
they're crisp, then crushes them and mixes them
with lavender. It sounds disgusting. I would

rather just suck lavender.

'If only there were snakes round here,' I told Nellie, 'I should be even richer, for the apothecary pays good money for adders.'

She shuddered, 'What does he do with snakes?'

'He dries them, grinds them into powder, and mixes in nearly a hundred different ingredients,' I told her. 'It cures the plague.'

Nellie shuddered again. So did I. We are all afraid of plague. It is a fearful disease, and everybody dreads the appearance of the plague doctor. He puts a huge bird-like mask over his head when he visits people with plague. The beak's packed full of herbs, so that's all he can smell.

Hey! Maybe it's smelly air that gives you the plague! No, it can't be. If it was, everyone I have ever met would be a corpse by now!

Nellie squeezed my hand. 'I will take your mice to the apothecary for you, John Bunn, if you will let me see your new animal.'

It is a porcupine. I have described it to her, but she says there is no such creature.

Bessie and I walked together into the city today, and saw a girl in the pillory. She was being punished for putting poison in her mistress's wine, and is to have an ear cut off. She's lucky. Last March a woman was boiled alive for the same crime. Better to have things thrown at you for a few days than to be cooked.

Bessie would not throw anything. She felt sorry for her.

'She's a poisoner,' I said, picking up a wrinkled apple that had bounced off the girl's head. 'A criminal.'

'I bet her mistress was horrible,' said Bessie. 'I'm lucky with mine.'

I wish I was lucky with my master. But even Scrope's not worth a week in the pillory.

It is a month since that warm day when I walked into the city with Bessie. Today is freezing cold and wet, with a wind that finds every hole in my clothes. No one wants dung on their gardens now, but I still have to shovel it up and take it to the manure pile which will soon be as big as Master Worsley's house.

The lions are bad-tempered in the cold. I'm afraid to go into the cages even when the beasts are on the upper level. I do not trust Scrope to keep them there. Yesterday he kept bawling, 'Faster, brat! I'm frozen!'

How does he think I felt? I was frozen *and* scared.

I hate winter. There is snow in the air. Father moans that he cannot keep warm. Bessie says if he moved a bit more he would be warmer. That makes him angry, but Bessie is able to go home. I must stay and listen to him grumble.

Today, Scrope left early, so I walked into the city to buy bread and a fine fish with my mouse money. Nellie spotted me as I hurried up Tower Hill. She is so small that her shawl wraps twice around her shivery little body.

'I'se coming, too, John Bunn,' she said, her teeth chattering like Tittle and Tattle's.

At the market, the bread seller was complaining at being outside in the cold. 'I'd rather be back in the bakery,' he moaned, 'but I'm the youngest apprentice so I get sent out when it's freezing.'

I asked, 'Is it warm in the bakery?' and he said they have two ovens! I should like to work there. 'Could I learn to bake bread?' I asked. 'Would they like a new boy?'

He laughed. 'They would not want one smelling of dung!'

Nellie threw a stone at him. 'John Bunn smells better'n your bread!' she cried.

On the way to Billingsgate market we passed

78

a group of apprentices keeping warm by kicking a ball of leather scraps tied together. The ball bounced off a doorway and rolled towards us. Nellie kicked it back.

The boys were having such fun. I wish I could be like them. There is no one of my age in the Tower. I was just plucking up courage to ask if I could play, when the master of one of them rushed out of his workshop and set about the boy with a thick stick. The others shook their fists at

the boy's master and called him names, so he set about them as well. Next thing, he was after me! I ran! Nellie followed, laughing. That warmed us up!

Snow has arrived.

Snow has lain thick on the ground for two weeks. We freeze at night. I'm wearing every bit of clothing I have, but I cannot get warm. I have stuffed old moss in my shoes, and still my toes are numb. I feel that if I hit them with a stone, they would shatter like glass. But at last the snow is melting. From our window I can see a pickpocket in St Katherine's stocks. He's been there since early morning, but it's too cold for people to stop to throw rubbish at him. Now it's almost dusk. I hope he will soon be freed. He cannot even stamp his bare feet to keep warm.

It has turned colder. The snow is freezing again. I took the pickpocket the last of my beer and bread.

He was blue with cold and couldn't hold my mug. I fed him small pieces of bread dipped in beer. While I was there, a bent old woman came out of a cottage with some rags to wrap his feet and hands. He managed to whisper, 'Bless you.'

The beasts came into my mind. I trudged through the snow to the Lion Tower, and found their water still frozen. It is colder inside those stone walls than outside.

I broke the ice with a chunk of rock. The animals are miserable. I wish I could wrap them in rags like the pickpocket's feet, but they are too dangerous. Anyway, all the rags I have are on my back. Tittle and Tattle huddle together for warmth

and Pooper is usually nowhere to be seen. Bessie told me she sometimes sees him in the Lieutenant's garden. Perhaps he finds shelter among the trees.

When I went home, the pickpocket had gone. I hope he did not die. But if he did, he will not be suffering any more.

After a few weeks of snow and ice, and slipping and shivering, spring is coming! The air doesn't bite my nose any more. Yesterday I delivered a small load of manure to a house I have not visited before. The gardener said the master would give me a penny if I spread the muck for him. I did so, and was rewarded with a pot of their own good beer and the tastiest pigeon pasty ever. All the while, the lady of the house sat at her window in the sunshine, sewing. Father says my mother used to sew baby clothes in the afternoons before I was born. That was when things were different, before Father was wounded and stopped working.

I hope I go to that house again.

Scrope was a beast today. No, worse than a beast. Our animals are never nasty just for the sake of it. If Scrope pokes them with his prodder, or if they're hungry, they get angry. But Scrope is often horrible to me for absolutely nothing. He dislikes his job, especially in winter, but he keeps it because it gives him ways of making extra money.

I have caught no mice at all these past weeks. Perhaps they found warmer places in the winter, like the grain storehouses down by the river. Now I have only one way of making extra money – by spreading muck. I hate my job. No, that's not true. I like working with the animals. I would like to be able to look after them properly, and keep the animals and their cages clean, so that when the king came, he would send for me and say, 'John Bunn, I am proud to let people come to see my beasts, because they look well and handsome.'

But Scrope spoils everything. Tomorrow, when he is out, I will go to Paul's Walk and try to get another job. But first I must go to the river and wash the animal smell off me.

I put on my cleanest clothes and walked to St Paul's Cathedral. I was quite warm by the time I reached the huge churchyard. Inside the great front door, I looked down the middle of the cathedral along Paul's Walk. Pickpockets and cutpurses

are all over the Walk, but I came because it is somewhere for servants to find new masters. I am sure I could be a good servant, but it seems nobody else thinks so. I went to Paul's Walk as a muckspreader, and that is how I came home.

It is so windy today. The beasts are restless. So is Scrope. I was fetching water for the wolf this morning, when Pooper dived down, knocking Scrope's hat off, and screeching, 'Slit yer throat!'

I got the blame, of course. My back is bruised, and my ears still burn where Scrope swiped them with his stick. But I feel better about that after what I saw on the way home.

A beggar was being whipped out of town. He eats soap, to make himself froth at the mouth, so people feel sorry for him. We have both been beaten today, yet I know who I would rather be. At least I have a job. And I have a family who care about me.

Today a young leopard arrived. The poor thing is terrified. It has had a long sea voyage, and now it has Scrope. He is angry because the beast clawed his shirt, and wants to stop giving it food and water. 'That will teach it a lesson,' he snarled.

I think the leopard is more likely to die.

When Scrope went home to get his sleeve mended (and have a jug of ale on the way, no doubt), I went to see Bessie. The cook was at the market, so I sat by the kitchen fire. One of the little maids gave me a plate of cold pheasant and some wine. Afterwards I had some marzipan, which is the sweetest thing I have ever tasted. It is

made with sugar, which costs a small fortune!

This is the life! If Scrope could see me now!

Today Scrope sent me off with a huge barrow-load of muck and, as I left, the rain began. It fell in torrents and hasn't stopped since. The streets are so slippery I was on my bottom three times before I got up Tower Hill. Then a farmer drove his horse and cart into my barrow. He stopped to pick me up, and looked as miserable as I felt.

'Sorry, lad,' he said. 'I dunno, it's dreadful . . .'

'What is?' I asked.

He pointed to his cart.

The poor man had brought his last lot of sheepskins to town to sell, and they were so wet and disgusting I doubt if he could give them away. I wonder which of us looked worse – him with his dripping load, or me with my barrow-load of muck, which was slowly being washed to the ground. (Not that I cared. Less to spread.)

The house I went to belongs to a Justice of the

Peace. He holds courts, like a judge, and is important and respected. While I was spreading his muck (for which I was paid a penny ha'penny!) I heard two different sounds. One was the pounding of the rain, and the other was music, which I liked better. I peeped through the window, but it had stopped.

A girl had a harp and a lute, but as I have never seen them played, I did not know which I heard. Imagine having music in your home, instead of listening to your father moaning about his life.

If I had an instrument, I'm sure I could play as well as the girl. Then I could give up my job and become a strolling player, or even a musician at the king's court!

Today I lost Father. I went home from work, worn out, hoping he had saved me some food. But he wasn't there. I called for Mother Moody, but she had not seen him since he went out in the early afternoon.

'He must be begging,' I said. 'He'll be caught one day, I know he will.'

'Not today,' said Mother Moody. 'I shared my dinner with him, so he is not hungry enough to beg.'

No, I thought, but he might be thirsty. I headed for the Sign of the Rose, our nearest tavern.

Father had not been there. That means he had no money. I had to find him before he was caught begging without a licence. I walked down little dark alleys that stunk of pee, in and out of taverns, along the river bank as far as London Bridge, then up New Fish Street. The light was fading, and I was scared to walk back the length of Thames Street in the dark, so I began to run.

The city is dangerous at night. You can get

bashed on the head and robbed before you hit the ground. There's never a watchman around when you want one. If he does find you and sets up a hue and cry, few people will be willing to join in and hunt down the villains. You'd never get your money back.

I wanted to see if Bessie had seen Father, but the Tower was locked for the night, so there was nothing for it but to hurry home.

I banged up the stairs in the darkness, counting out loud, 'Thirteen, fourteen, jump, sixteen, jump, eighteen . . .' and made it safely to the top.

There, on his bed, was Father. I blinked, wondering if I was going mad and he had been there all along.

'Where . . .?' I began.

'I went to look for work,' he growled, and turned to face the wall.

Could it be true? If so, he was disappointed.

There was a strong smell of ale in the room.

Father is miserable. I stay out as long as possible now the evenings are light. It means putting up with Nellie's chatter and pleas to see the beasts again, but at least she is cheerful.

Father does not move from his bed. If it was not for the little money I earn and the food Bessie brings, he would starve and die. Mother Moody says he is ashamed that he cannot feed his family as he used to do.

It is two weeks since Father has moved from his bed, but today something happened that made him sit up. King Henry came to the Tower! His barge moored alongside the wharf today. I was on the high walkway fetching a dead pigeon for the leopard, so I saw everything!

The king arrived from Greenwich. He travels by river when he can. Even though the Thames is busy, it's not as crowded as the streets. There were halberdiers guarding him, and trumpeters announced his arrival. The king took his party of friends straight to the Lord Lieutenant's house.

Perhaps Bessie saw him! Maybe she even

gave him his dinner!

I wondered if he'd come to the menagerie. Scrope was wondering, too – he went twitchy again! He told me to make sure that Tittle and Tattle were out of sight every moment the king was here. And I was to keep Pooper quiet. But Pooper was nowhere to be seen.

Later the king did come to the menagerie! He spoke to me! Well, he didn't really, but I heard him speak, and I was as close to him as I am to Father at night in our little attic room! Maybe not quite that close.

I kept back against the wall, clutching my shovel. The men held handkerchiefs to their noses, and the ladies held pomanders. It could not have been me they were smelling, not from that distance. It was probably just the animal smell.

The most important lady in the party was called Katherine, Lady Latimer. The king likes her a *lot*. She made a big fuss about how powerful and handsome the lion, Henry, is (the new Henry, that is), and the king liked that, too.

Suddenly, he said, 'The monkeys, keeper. Where are the monkeys?'

'M-m-monkeys, Your Majesty?' said Scrope, bowing so low I thought his nose would scrape the floor.

'Yes, the m-m-monkeys,' said the king, and he looked round at his friends, who laughed. I think it's important to laugh at a king's jokes, however bad they are.

Scrope pretended to remember. 'Oh! The monkeys. This way, Your Royal Majesty.'

The ladies' skirts gathered a deep fringe of dirt as they swept towards the monkey room. Once everyone was inside, I ran to the door and peeped through the crack where the hinges are.

Lady Katherine liked the monkeys, especially

Tittle. 'Charming!' she said. 'What is its name?'

The king is a fast thinker, I'll say that. As quick as blinking, he replied, 'She is called Kate. Is that not so, keeper?'

Scrope bent double. 'Y-yes, Your Majesty, Sire.'

Lady Katherine went pink. She thought the monkey was named after her! 'A pretty compliment, Sire,' she said. 'May I stroke her?'

Ha! Scrope went to pick her up, but Tittle swung up out of his way. Go to Scrope? Not likely!

The king began to tap his foot. 'Come along, man,' he said.

Scrope had no choice. 'John Bunn?' he called.

I leapt through the door. 'Here, Master Scrope.'

The ladies jammed their pomanders against their noses. I whistled, and Tittle swooped down to my shoulder and gripped my neck. Lady Katherine stepped forward to stroke her. Her fingers didn't actually touch the fur, but the king didn't notice. He was too busy watching the delight on Lady Katherine's face. I wonder if it was real delight.

As they left, a fat man pressed a few extra coins into Scrope's sweaty hand. Suddenly I spotted Pooper toddling along the cobbles near the gate. I held my breath, but the parrot watched quietly, his head on one side. The fat man was last to pass through the gate and, as he did, Pooper opened his beak and squawked, 'Fustilugs!'

I ducked out of sight. The fat man turned, his face purple, and strode back to Scrope. 'Insolent wretch!' He snatched the purse from him, and left.

What a day! Father is so jealous. He will never see the king so close.

Next day

I would not tell anyone, but I cried tonight.

Earlier, Master Worsley called me to his office

– well, to the door of his office – and told me that the king is giving Tittle (he called her 'Kate') to Lady Katherine, as a gift.

What can I do? As the monkeys are in the king's menagerie, he considers they are his. I must get Tittle clean and brushed, and ready to leave the Lion Tower in two days' time.

Two days later

I put poor Tittle into a cage on the back of a cart today. She looked sad, and I know I did, too, because Scrope told me to do something about my face before I turned the milk sour.

He loaded a basket of food and a heap of extra straw on the cart, took up the reins and was gone – off to the king's great palace of Hampton Court, where Lady Katherine is staying.

I followed them to the Bulwark Gate and watched until I could no longer see Tittle's tiny paws clutching the bars of her wooden prison.

99

I do not know where Nellie comes from, but I was glad to feel her little hand slip into mine.

The only good thing about yesterday was that Scrope was away. Bessie came to the menagerie in the afternoon. She had heard about Tittle going, and knew I would be sad. She brought strawberries for Tattle and Pooper.

Tattle would not eat.

I will never see Tittle again. She was one of the few living beings who does not mind being close to me.

Today was so hot. I worry about Tittle – if Scrope is being nice to her. No, he's never been nice to anyone or anything in his life. I invited Nellie in for the afternoon. I needed her help. We fetched many buckets of water to throw over the

animals. That cooled them down, and I think they enjoyed it.

Scrope will soon return, and we shall be back to normal.

Something terrible has happened! Early this afternoon, Scrope returned in a panic. He said that as he neared Hampton Court, he stopped to check that Tittle was clean enough to be presented to Lady Katherine. As he opened the cage, Tittle bounded over his shoulder and ran towards a small wood. He tried for two days to catch her but couldn't. Well, of course. He is so cruel – what animal would go to him willingly?

Then Scrope said something that excited and terrified me.

'John Bunn, you must go to Hampton Court, catch the monkey, and present it to Lady Katherine. It ran to a copse of trees with a giant oak that's split by lightning. Hurry. Get going, dolt!'

'Alone?' I gasped.

'I cannot come,' he said. 'I must look after the beasts.'

Huh! I know why he will not come. If Tittle is lost, it will be my fault. Scrope won't want to be around if the king finds out Lady Katherine's present has run away. I am to be the sacrifice – unless I can catch Tittle.

I raced home to tell Father. He was so excited that he came downstairs to see me off. 'My boy going to a royal palace!' he said. 'My life might have come to nothing, but this is your chance to do something worthwhile.'

As I hurried away, shouting, 'Goodbye!', I looked back. I may have been mistaken, but it seemed to me that Father almost smiled.

I cannot raise a smile. All I foresee is trouble if I do not find Tittle. I filled my pocket with her favourite food, and stuffed her collar and lead inside my shirt.

I had never driven the cart before, so Scrope

sent for the Tower scavenger to drive me through the busy streets. Once we were out of London, I was to take over and the scavenger would make his way back. His job is to walk the Tower, clearing up filth and finding useful things, and he seldom escapes the great walls, so he was glad of the trip.

Scrope sniggered. 'You are two of a kind,' he said. 'Both stinkers.'

At the last minute, Bessie appeared and thrust a basket on the cart. 'Food and drink,' she panted, then, seeing my alarmed face, added, 'With the cook's blessing!'

I was glad she wasn't giving me stolen food in front of Scrope.

The city streets were busy, and sometimes we were unable to move for sheep going to market. Once over the bridge it was clearer. When we reached a quiet country lane, the scavenger stopped. I was sure I could manage the horse and cart now.

I thanked him and he set off back to the Tower. The horse plodded on. Most people I passed said a cheery, 'Good day!' They must have wondered why I had an empty cage and a heap of straw on my cart.

I was just beginning to enjoy the ride, when I nearly leapt off the cart in terror. Something was touching my back!

'Hello, John Bunn,' said a voice.

Nellie! She scrambled up beside me. 'It was so warm in that straw I fell asleep,' she said. 'Where's we off to?'

She was beside herself with excitement when she learned we were going to a royal palace. I could hardly send her back, and her mother would probably not notice she was gone. Truth to tell, I was glad of her company.

I looked for somewhere to stop for the night. The track ran alongside a stream, and when we came upon a good-sized farmhouse, I decided it was best to stay nearby.

I tied the horse to my foot, so he would not be stolen, and shared my supper with Nellie. I expect to reach Hampton Court tomorrow, so we ate well, saving a little bread and ham for breakfast.

The countryside was dark, like ink. There were animals in the undergrowth – I could hear them. Strange that I am more scared of wild pigs and snakes than I am of a lion.

I was right to be afraid. There was a crashing noise right in front of us and I found myself staring at a wild boar! I yelled and swung my

lantern at it. Nellie screamed. When I looked again, it was gone. I wondered would I ever sleep? Did Tittle feel as lonely and afraid as I did?

I should have tied the horse to a tree, not to my foot. I didn't realise that he does not care to curl up as dogs do, but likes to walk about. I ended up much nearer the stream than when I went to sleep. I was lucky not to end up in it. I finally woke, damp and stiff, as dawn was breaking. Nellie snuffled nearby, cosy under her straw.

After breakfast, we harnessed the horse –
with difficulty, for it was my first time – and set
off again.

It was a busy road, and wide, too. I let the
horse follow the track and relaxed, enjoying
the sunshine. Nellie leaned against me.

I was drifting in and out of sleep, when suddenly – I found myself in a ditch! The stupid
horse must have wandered off the road, and now
the cart is one wheel short. Nellie is fine, but
Tittle's cage is lying in ditchwater.

What on earth was I going to do?

Then a little sharp-faced dog came along the track, closely followed by a young boy. He carried a stick and two dead rabbits. His dinner, I suppose.

'Summat 'appened, eh?' he said cheerily.

Well, obviously.

He peered into the ditch. 'What you got in that cage, then?'

'Fleas,' Nellie said. 'He catches fleas. For flea circuses.'

'Oooh,' he said. 'Is they drownded?'

'No,' she said. 'They all escaped.'

He eyed the broken cartwheel. 'You won't fix that,' he said.

He was right. We would have to leave the cart and cage, and keep moving. I was on an important errand.

'I must go,' I said, looking down my nose at the boy. 'I am on a mission for King Henry.'

The boy stared, then hooted with laughter – so hard he could hardly speak. 'Flea catcher to His

Majesty, are you? Ha! Ha! Ha!' And off he went, swinging his mangy rabbits.

Nellie ran a short way after him. 'Fat head!' she bellowed.

We walked on, leading the horse, and after a while we were overtaken by a woman on a donkey. She stopped and looked back. 'Why don't you ride your horse? 'Tis a good walk to Clappeham.'

I felt stupid. That had never occurred to me. It wasn't easy getting on, but eventually I was astride. I pulled Nellie up behind me. She is as light as swans' feathers.

We passed through the village of Clappeham, and on through the countryside. We stopped at a stream to let the horse drink. The water was delicious – streams are so clear outside London. I was just struggling on the horse again, when I heard snorting. Nellie clutched me and I turned, terrified it was some wild animal, but it was a charcoal burner – laughing at me!

He invited us to eat with him, and gave us a leg of chicken to share. 'Don't ask me where I got the bird,' he said, winking. We didn't care!

He gave us directions to Wandsworth, where we crossed the River Wandle. We stopped near some small cottages to try to buy food there. I had a few pennies in my pocket.

What luck! I found a kind couple at one of the cottages. The man is a farm worker who earns very little. He has children to feed, so his wife earns extra money by brewing her own ale to sell to the local people.

It is the best I ever tasted, and she would not take a penny for it, or for our food! Poor people, like this alewife and the charcoal burner, are often the most generous.

The farm worker said I could sleep in the cowshed. Nellie was offered a bed on the floor with the couple's own children, but she wanted to stay with me. I told them where I was going, and why. The woman was curious. 'What is a monkey?' she asked. 'A sort of donkey?'

Nellie explained. I could see it made her feel important to know so much. When she talked about the rest of the king's beasts, it was obvious that the woman thought she was a simpleton, imagining things. This couple have never travelled further than the nearest market town.

I had such a comfortable night's sleep and felt ready for anything when I woke. For our journey, we were given a loaf of bread, a chunk of cheese, two onions and some radishes. I thanked the couple. Nellie hugged them.

Later in the day we reached the village of Kingston. A fine wooden bridge crossed the river, which I was amazed to discover was the Thames. Can it possibly be the same river as flows past the Tower?

We plodded over rolling countryside, with woods, pasture and meadowas far as the eye could see.

Then straight ahead was the largest house I have ever seen. Hampton Court. Nellie's mouth dropped open and stayed open.

But I had no time to waste. We had to find a small copse with a lightning-split oak tree. Scrope had described it well, and we soon found it. I led Nellie, on the horse, into the wood. Tittle would not be afraid of them. She's used to lions!

I whistled.

Silence. Even the birds were quiet.

I whistled again. And again.

Chitter-chatter-chitter-chatter! Racing through the undergrowth towards me was Tittle! She leapt into my arms and I hugged her and hugged her.

Although we were so close to Hampton Court, I could not bear to part with Tittle so soon. We stayed in the wood for the night. Tittle curled up in my arms, but she had her little collar and lead on. I dared not risk losing her. Imagine the king's anger!

It took until midday dinner time (and we had nothing to eat) to convince the king's guards that I was telling the truth. The first one who stopped us shouted to another, 'Smelly brat here with a furry thing clinging to 'is leg, an' 'e says the king ordered it for milady Latimer!'

A group of soldiers gathered round, and a groom took the horse away.

An officer came to investigate. He listened to my story and said, 'Yes, I remember. The monkey was due here days ago, His Majesty's serving

man said. Well, better tell Her Ladyship.'

'Where do I find her?' I asked.

'Not you, lad,' said the officer. 'I'll take you to the stables. That's the place for animals.'

As there was only one animal in sight – Tittle – I took that as an insult.

'I'll see that Her Ladyship is informed,' said the officer, when we reached the stables. 'His Majesty's not here.'

Nellie and I waited all day. A stable boy called Dickon took me to the kitchen to get some food. They wouldn't let me in, but I didn't care. I just stared. I've never seen anywhere so vast or so busy.

We were given huge slices of pie and a loaf each, and Dickon pilfered some fruit and nuts – even I did not see him do it! So Nellie, Tittle and I were full, and we had a bed of fresh straw to sleep on. Heaven!

We waited all next day for the Lady Latimer. Now that her husband is dead, some here call her

Katherine Parr, which is her former name. It must be confusing having different names. Plain John Bunn is enough for me. I fell asleep that night wondering how Pooper and Tattle were.

Then next day, she came! Not to the stables, of course. She was in the garden, and sent for me.

Lady Katherine stared at the monkey. She didn't look at it the way she did when the king was with her. I don't think she likes Tittle at all. She made no move to stroke her.

One of her women said, 'His Majesty will be here soon, madam.'

'I know,' said Lady Katherine. 'I suppose I must keep this smelly brute.'

'It is His Majesty's gift,' said the woman.

Lady Katherine said, 'Ugh,' swung her skirts and stalked away.

She doesn't want Tittle. I don't want her to have Tittle. I am afraid Lady Katherine might let her escape or, worse, keep her and neglect her.

We waited another two days. I amused

myself by watching what goes on around the great palace. Nellie made friends with the gardeners, and nibbled at strawberries and early blackcurrants and raspberries all day. Suddenly, while Tittle was drinking at the river, there was a great to-do. Gentlemen and ladies appeared from all directions. King Henry's barge was near!

I grabbed Tittle, raced back to the stables and ripped up a clump of grass to groom her with. Then we waited outside for the king and Lady Katherine to appear.

Of course they didn't.

The stable boys laughed. 'Big King Hal will need to fill his belly after the journey from Whitehall.'

Dickon sniggered. 'He needs to fill his belly after a stroll round the gardens!'

I liked those boys, and ate my dinner with them. Nellie sat nearby. They were full of gossip, and said the king wants a new wife, and his eye was on Lady Katherine Parr.

'Surely she would not marry someone as old and fat as the king?' I said.

'Old and fat and smelly,' the head lad, Tom, replied. 'Oh, sorry, John Bunn – nothing wrong with being smelly,' he said. 'It's his leg that smells – they say it's rotten with disease.'

'Anyway, she has no choice,' said Dickon. 'What the king wants, he gets. He's had five wives already!'

Lady Katherine and the king never came, so I spent the afternoon helping Dickon groom the horses. They take such care of their animals at Hampton Court – dogs, horses, hunting birds.

I wish we treated the king's beasts as well. They should not be stuffed into small cages and left, so that their coats grow dirty and matted.

What a day! The King and Lady Katherine suddenly

arrived in the stable yard, dressed for hunting. Dickon, Tom and the other stable boys rushed round like mad, making everything ready.

I watched from the doorway, Nellie hiding behind me and Tittle on my shoulder. She chattered so loudly the king heard her.

'Ah! Come, my lady,' he boomed. 'Your new friend has arrived. Shall we let Kate talk to Kate?' He looked round to make sure everyone was laughing at his joke. They were.

The king looked at Tittle. 'She is not as lively as when we saw her before.'

She was probably scared stiff of this huge man. Or maybe I had overfed her.

The king frowned. 'Boy!' he said. 'What have you done to Kate that she is become so dull?'

All the good Hampton Court food must have fed my brain, because, quick as a blink, I replied, 'She has left her mate back at the Tower, Sire.' I took a deep breath. 'Kate would much rather be with her Hal.'

'Heh? Kate's mate is Hal?' said the king. His piglike eyes sparkled at Lady Katherine. 'What think you . . . Kate?'

Katherine Parr's brain works fast, too. She glanced down and murmured quietly, so I had to strain to hear, 'Perhaps everyone would be happy if Kate were with . . . Hal.'

The king didn't say a word. He just gazed at her, then gently took her arm and walked away.

They had forgotten Tittle. Now what? I decided to stay with her until she was taken from me.

Last night, the gossip was all about the king hoping to marry Lady Katherine. Poor woman. I would rather live with Tittle than with the king.

I had just fetched breakfast from the kitchen for me and Nellie when a message came from Lady Katherine's serving-woman. I was to return Tittle to the Tower! But this time by boat – on Lady Katherine's orders!

And once we were back, Scrope would not

even listen. He ranted on all afternoon about how I made a mess of the simple matter of delivering a gift. He forgot that *he* lost the gift in the first place.

I spent two hours shovelling muck, and knowing I had to start again at dawn next day. Scrope had not lifted a spade since I left. It was a miracle the animals had even been fed.

Two days of shifting mountains of dung and washing down the yard to make it fit for visitors!

Master Worsley arrived after midday dinner (which I did not have time to finish). No sooner was he in his house than he sent for Scrope.

Scrope was in there but a second or two, then came out and bellowed, 'John Bunn! *Here!*'

Pooper took up the cry, 'John Bunn! Here!' he squawked. 'Dolt!'

Scrope threw a stone at the poor parrot, and ordered me to Master Worsley's door, cuffing my ears as I passed.

My stomach sank into my hose. I must, I thought, be in terrible trouble. Then, when I was called inside, I *knew* I was.

Master Worsley spoke. 'The Lady Katherine instructs that Kate and Hal – monkeys, apparently – are to be in the special care of Keeper John Bunn. She and His Majesty wish to be kept informed of their wellbeing. You are therefore promoted to the post of Beast Keeper, alongside Master Scrope. Bear in mind, John Bunn, that this is a royal appointment, for the Lady Katherine and His Majesty are to marry.'

I left Master Worsley's house in a daze. I am not John Bunn the muckspreader any more, I thought. I am John Bunn, Beast Keeper to His Majesty. And, best of all, Scrope can no longer beat me and treat me badly and swear at me, for I am his equal!

Scrope was so angry. He thumped the floor with his prodder, banged the cage bars and stabbed it into the ground.

Except he missed the ground and got his foot. Huzzah! Prodded by his own prodder!

Oh, this is the best day of my life! I am *somebody*. What more could I possibly want?

Later

I have thought a lot, and I have promised myself that I will look after the king's beasts well. He will be proud of them. Tittle and Tattle are back together. They need no longer be hidden, because the king accepts that they are his. And Nellie may visit whenever I please. I am happy.

It is true! The king has proposed to Lady Katherine, and she has accepted. This, on my first day as Beast Keeper!

If only I did not feel so odd. I wonder if I have a sickness coming upon me. Yet I do not feel ill – far from it! This is the greatest day of my life.

Scrope limped over to me after midday dinner. He wasn't friendly in the least, but he wasn't rude, either.

'Someone must shift the muck,' he said. 'Will you?'

'No,' I said. 'I am not a muckspreader any more. We –' I actually said 'we'! '– we must find someone else to do it.'

'That will be difficult,' said Scrope. 'It is a dirty job, and sometimes dangerous.'

Oh, really?

'No,' he continued, 'it is not everyone's idea

of a good job. We –' *He* said 'we' this time! '– we need someone with guts, who does not mind the stink.'

As soon as Scrope said that, I knew. Someone who was fearless, who would not mind the stink . . . would not even notice it . . .

I ran home and leapt up the stairs, bouncing off Ma Moody who was slowly climbing up ahead of me, counting, 'Sixteen, u-up, eighteen, nineteen, u-up'. I hopped about waiting for her to get out of the way, then plunged straight through number twenty-one! That is not like me – I never make mistakes on the stairs.

But I was so excited, I did not stop to see if I was cut. I bounded on and at last I burst through our door.

'Father, get up!' I yelled. 'I've got you a job!'

'Twenty-two, twenty-three, u-up,' Toby heard. His brain felt woolly. He shook his head to clear it, then looked around. Yep, fairies on the walls.

'I'm me again. No lions, no dung, no fleas in my bed. Just me, Toby Tucker.'

For a few moments, he stared at the wooden chest, remembering when he had been John Bunn, his ancestor from nearly five hundred years ago. It was mind-blowing! He wondered if he would ever get used to the awesome power of his wooden chest.

He heard a snuffle. It was Snowball, still lying

in the doorway. Toby was about to send her down-stairs, when he suddenly changed his mind. He didn't know why. 'Here, Snowball,' he said.

She bounced over to him.

'Want to play?'

Snowball barked, and followed him down-stairs to the garden. Toby tried to teach her to fetch. She was hopeless. It ended up with Toby doing the fetching while she wagged her pom-pom tail.

Afterwards, they went upstairs, Toby to watch a DVD and Snowball to snooze on the floor beside him.

Half an hour later, Toby heard the car. Leaving Snowball asleep, he went downstairs and found Evie unpacking her shopping.

Was this the right moment to talk about his secret? He took a deep breath. 'Do you believe in magic?' he asked.

Evie snorted. 'The only magic I know about is the disappearing trick Don does whenever I want him to help with the cooking. Here, take these doggie chews.'

Toby examined them. 'This one's a bit big for Snowball,' he said. 'Oh! I nearly forgot! How's your mum?'

'She'll be fine,' said Evie happily. 'Not as mobile as she was, but she'll be able to walk OK. Toby, I have good news for you!'

'What?'

'We realise Snowball's not really a boy's sort of dog,' said Evie, 'so we've asked my mum's neighbour if he'll swap. He's going to have Snowball, and we'll have Barney. Look!'

Outside in the garden, jumping excitedly round Don, was a jet-black Labrador.

'Barney!' Toby ran outside.

'Hope you like him,' said Don.

'He's great!'

said Toby, happily scratching behind the dog's ears.

Don grunted. 'I reckon Evie's planning to talk me into keeping him even after her mum gets out of hospital. She's worried he'll be too much for her to cope with.'

'Evie will, won't she?' said Toby. 'Talk you into it, I mean?'

Don sighed. 'Probably. At least her mum can see him whenever she wants.'

Toby was thrilled. He'd be able to take this dog for walks, no problem. 'Can I take him to Jake's?' he asked.

But just then, Evie rushed out. 'Snowball's gone!' she cried. 'I can't find her anywhere!'

Toby grinned. 'She's asleep in my room. I'll get her.'

He fetched Snowball and put the sleepy dog down on the grass. She saw Barney at the same time as Barney saw her. That woke her up! The two dogs went mad, jumping round each other,

barking themselves silly.

'Don,' said Toby, 'it'd be mean to have Barney and not Snowball. They'd miss each other terribly.'

'Eh?'

'Well, animals have feelings, too,' said Toby.

'I'll think about it,' Don grunted. 'Go and show Barney to your mates.'

Toby went indoors to get a lead. He thought of John Bunn, and how badly he wanted his animals to have just a little bit of freedom.

'Evie,' he said. 'I think I'll take Snowball out,

too. She'll like that.'

After all, he thought, she's been cooped up all day, and that's not good for animals.

Especially lions!

 **Who Will**

TOBY TUCKER

be next?

He's Seti, keeping sneaky secrets in Ancient Egypt!

He's Niko, dodging the donkey doo in Ancient Greece!

He's Titus, sludging through the sewer in Ancient Rome!

He's Alfie Trott, picking people's pockets in Victorian London!

He's Fred Barrow, hogging all the pig swill in wartime London!

EGMONT PRESS: ETHICAL PUBLISHING

Egmont Press is about turning writers into successful authors and children into passionate readers – producing books that enrich and entertain. As a responsible children's publisher, we go even further, considering the world in which our consumers are growing up.

Safety First
Naturally, all of our books meet legal safety requirements. But we go further than this; every book with play value is tested to the highest standards – if it fails, it's back to the drawing-board.

Made Fairly
We are working to ensure that the workers involved in our supply chain – the people that make our books – are treated with fairness and respect.

Responsible Forestry
We are committed to ensuring all our papers come from environmentally and socially responsible forest sources.

For more information, please visit our website at
www.egmont.co.uk/ethicalpublishing